The Warthog's Tail

Debby Atwell

Houghton Mifflin Company Boston 2005

Walter Lorraine Books

Walter Lorraine (wn) Books

www.houghtonmifflinbooks.com

Library of Congress Cataloging-in-Publication Data

Atwell, Debby.
 The warthog's tail / by Debby Atwell.
      p. cm.
 "Walter Lorraine books."
 Summary: Impatient to go trick-or-treating, a young witch tries her mother's spells
on a warthog without success, until a mysterious old man teaches her the art of persuasion.
 ISBN–13: 978-0-618-50781-8 (hardcover)
 ISBN–10: 0-618-50781-7 (hardcover)
[1. Witches—Fiction. 2. Mothers and daughters—Fiction. 3. Behavior—Fiction. 4. Warthog—Fiction.
5. Halloween—Fiction.]
I. Title.
 PZ7.A8935War 2005
 [E]—dc22
                                                                                200500055

Printed in Singapore
TWP   10 9 8 7 6 5 4 3 2 1

To Steve Burke

Tegan, the witch's daughter, hurried home with a bucket of
water. She must not be late, for tonight was Trick or Treat.
But what was this? A gigantic sleeping warthog blocked
the gate to her house.
"What should I do to get rid of this nasty tusked beast?" Tegan
wondered. "Mother says I am still too young to cast spells, but I
am afraid to go near him."

Tegan decided she would have to try to cast a spell rather than wake the warthog.

So when a dog appeared walking down the road, Tegan said in her typical bossy way:

"*Dog, dog bite warthog so I can get home in time for Trick or Treat.*"

But of course the magic did not work and the dog said no.

Tegan stubbornly picked up a stick and said the magic words:
   "Stick, stick beat dog. Dog, dog bite warthog so I can get
home in time for Trick or Treat."
   But the stick didn't like being bossed around either and said no.

Tegan took one of her mother's magical matches she had hidden in her pocket and said the magic words:

"*Match, match burn stick. Stick, stick beat dog. Dog, dog bite warthog so I can get home in time for Trick or Treat.*"

But match said, "Bossy little witch, you're not supposed to play with your mother's matches!"

Tegan did not know what to do.

Just then, an old man came walking down the road.

"What's the matter, little witch?" he asked.

Tegan said, "I can't get rid of this dangerous warthog with my magic words. Tonight is Halloween, and it's time for Trick or Treat."

The old man replied, "If the magic won't work, why don't you try persuasion?"

"How do I try persuasion?" asked Tegan.

"Speak politely, put a little heart in your smile, and then . . . just trust."

Then the old man asked Tegan if she would persuade the rock in the field to roll over so he could sit down for a bit.

Tegan walked into the field. "Mr. Rock," she said politely, "would you please roll over by the old man? He needs to sit down." Then she put a little heart in her smile and just trusted.

The rock said, "Sure. Just give me a cushion of the horse's hay to lie on."

Tegan went up to a horse in the field.

"Hey," said the horse, who had seen and heard everything, "I like your style, kid witch. Take all the hay you need. And might I get a drink of that water in your bucket?" The horse smiled a most charming smile and just trusted.

"Why, of course," Tegan answered.

The rock lay on the hay, the horse sipped the water, and the old man
sat down.

"Do you have a match so I can light my pipe?" the old man asked.
Tegan politely handed the old man her match and said, "Old man, after
you light your pipe, would you please throw the match at the stick so
that it will jump and hit the dog, and the dog will bite the warthog, and
then I can get home in time for Trick or Treat?" Then she put a little
heart in her smile and just trusted.

19

The old man nodded politely. "It would be an honor to help you," he said. Then he lit his pipe. He tossed the match at the stick and—kaboom!—the match began to burn the stick, and the stick began to beat the dog.

The dog began to bite the nasty warthog's tail. Off came the tail.
The warthog ran away.

Tegan picked up the bucket of water and thanked the old man
for his help.

"Take the warthog's tail," said the old man. "It may be valuable."

Tegan took the tail and ran home.

Tegan hid the warthog's tail in the closet. Soon, Tegan's mother
appeared, most upset.

"Oh, dear Tegan, we are simply doomed!" she wailed. "I must
have a fierce warthog tail for the Halloween spell. Alas! Without
one, there will be no Halloween ever again in the whole wide world!"

As you might guess, Tegan fetched the warthog's tail from the closet. "Look," she said. Her mother gasped. "It's a warthog's tail! Who gave this to you?" Tegan said, "The warthog himself! Please, Mom, now you can do the spell and Halloween will be all right. Then can we go trick or treating?" She put a little bit of you-know-what in her smile and just trusted.

"Yes, of course," said her mother. "Run and get into your costume!"

While Tegan got into her rabbit suit, she thought about the wise old man and his lesson about persuasion.

"Poor Mom doesn't understand," Tegan sighed.

When she was ready to go, Tegan looked everywhere for her mother. Finally, she called into her mother's darkened bedroom.

"Are you there, Mom?"

"Wait there, dear," chirped her mom. "I'm just putting an old costume away. I'll be right with you."